MW01120835

THE PROMISE
BOOK EIGHT OF THE CRAFTERS' CLUB SERIES

AN UNOFFICIAL MINECRAFT NOVEL

LOUISE GUY

Copyright © Louise Guy 2016.
First edition: 2016.
Printed by Go Direct Publishing Pty Ltd.

Print ISBN: 978-0-9944482-4-8

Edited by Kathy Betts
Cover design by Lana Pecherczyk
Cover illustration by Navid Bulbulija

For the real-life JJ and Jamie.

CHAPTER ONE

Trusting Sam

Jamie opened his eyes and smiled. His bedroom curtain flapped gently in the cool morning breeze allowing light to stream in through a gap. He listened as his brother turned over in the bunk above him. It was early, JJ would be asleep for ages. His older brother loved to sleep in.

Jamie thought about the day before. He'd had an awesome birthday. He had been sure it was going to be ruined by the arrival of his cousin, Sam, but instead it had turned into another thrilling adventure in the Minecraft world.

While Sam chose to lock himself away and watch television, the Crafters' Club members used the opportunity to re-enter the Minecraft world and give Jamie his birthday gift—a map they'd created especially for him.

The birthday celebrations had abruptly ended when Sam, playing from the Xbox, had used his Minecraft character to set off an explosion and attack them. The Crafters' Club members had been forced into situations they'd never encountered before while desperately trying to keep the portal a secret. They'd finally outwitted Sam and returned to the real world but, much to their dismay,

Sam discovered the portal in the forest. They made a promise that they would take Sam into the Minecraft world on one condition—that he kept the portal secret.

Jamie pushed his feet into the mattress of the bunk above him. "Come on bro', time to wake up. We've got a promise to keep, remember?"

JJ groaned. "There's no hurry, I'm still asleep."

Jamie laughed. "No you're not. Now get up. We need to find Sam and plan which map we're going to take him into."

"You find him," JJ said. "He's probably still asleep. The girls won't be ready yet, either, it's too early."

"I bet he's awake," Jamie said. "He'll be too excited to sleep."

"Fine, you talk to him and work out which map he'd like to visit. Store inventory and supplies and, after breakfast when the girls arrive, we can discuss going back in. We're going to have to make some pretty strict rules so he doesn't do anything stupid."

Jamie grinned as the rustle of blankets above him and a yawn signaled the conversation was over. He couldn't wait to go back through the portal. They'd need to work out a way to ensure Sam listened to them and respected the Minecraft world and its people. Sam had promised to follow their rules the day before, but their cousin was older and thought he knew everything. He also lied, a lot.

❧

Jamie pushed open the door to JJ's bedroom to see if Sam was still asleep. His cousin's bag had exploded. Clothes and magazines lay strewn across the floor, desk, and bed. JJ was not going to be happy that he had let Sam use his room. The bed was a mess of clothes and screwed-up bedding, but otherwise it was empty.

Jamie made his way to the kitchen. He expected to find his cousin eating breakfast. Instead he found his dad alone at the kitchen counter reading the paper. His dad threw the paper down and, jumping up from his chair, pulled Jamie into a bear hug.

"Hey, there's my eight-year-old champ. Have you recovered from your big birthday yet?"

Jamie laughed and struggled out of his father's arms. "Yeah, it was a great day. Awesome, in fact. Best birthday ever."

His dad grinned. "I'm glad. I'm about to cook some croissants if you're ready for breakfast?"

Jamie shook his head. "No thanks, maybe later. Have you seen Sam?"

"Sam? If he's not in bed I'd try the family room. He's probably in there watching TV."

"Okay, thanks." Jamie made his way back to the family room. He pushed open the door but the room was empty. He was about to leave when the television caught his eye. A Minecraft map filled the screen. He moved closer. The screen showed a familiar, hilly landscape leading to a village in the distance. Toby's village.

Jamie's heart raced. Surely Sam wouldn't have gone in alone? He picked up a controller and changed the view. A Minecraft character appeared. The familiar red-and-white checkered grin of Sam's character, OarsumBoss, was instantly recognizable. His red-and-black warrior skin contrasted with the greens and blues of the Minecraft world and he held a diamond sword out in front. Jamie watched OarsumBoss move toward the village, occasionally slashing his sword to cut grass or a tree. Jamie's eyes remained fixed on the screen. Not only had Sam worked out how to access inventory but the diamond sword confirmed he *had* inventory. It wasn't always the case when they entered the Minecraft world.

Jamie threw the controller down and ran to get JJ.

⚜

JJ, Annie, Charli, and Jamie crowded together on the couch in the family room, their eyes glued to the television screen. After waking JJ, Jamie had run next door to get Charli, and across the road to collect Annie.

"Why didn't he wait until we could all go in together?" Annie asked. "We could have helped him, shown him how everything works."

Charli laughed. "Doesn't look like he needed us to. He's holding a sword and right now he looks like he's sprinting. Not as dumb as we thought."

"Hopefully he'll be killed," JJ said. "Then he'll end up back out here and won't be able to re-enter. That's probably the best we can hope for."

Jamie shook his head. "No, we can't let that happen. He'll come straight out and tell Dad, then we'll never get to go back in. Not only that, he's heading to Toby's village. Who knows what damage he's going to do."

"Jamie's right," Annie said. "We need to go in and teach him how to exist in the Minecraft world, how to respect our friends who live there. We promised."

JJ snorted. "I don't think we need to worry about any promise we made. He certainly hasn't kept his word."

"It doesn't mean we should break our promise," Jamie said. "Come on, let's store some inventory. We need to be quick and get there before he causes trouble."

Annie sniffed and looked toward the family-room door. "What's that amazing smell?"

"My dad's cooking croissants," Jamie said. "We'll eat them later, we don't have time now."

"Are we all going in?" Annie asked.

Surprise registered on Jamie's face. He stopped loading inventory into the chests and turned to face Annie. "Of course, unless you don't want to?"

Annie's cheeks reddened. "It might be safer if I stay out and watch from here. If you get into danger I can help, perhaps even change the map. That worked yesterday."

"That's a great idea," JJ said. "But are you sure? I'm happy to stay out here if you'd prefer to go in."

Annie shook her head. "No. I'll stay."

Charli inhaled and laughed. "I think Annie's decision to stay has more to do with the wafting smell of buttery croissants than her desire to save us."

Annie laughed. "Okay, so maybe it helped me with my decision. But he's not my cousin. He'll listen to JJ."

JJ snorted again. "I doubt it."

They watched as Jamie moved his

character to place chests full of armor, weapons, and food in the map. He'd stayed out of sight of OarsumBoss who had just entered the village.

"Okay, all done," Jamie said. "Let's go in before he causes any problems."

"Too late," Charli said.

They watched as OarsumBoss used his sword to smash crops in the vegetable gardens. Villagers were moving quickly toward their huts.

Annie gasped. "What if he tries to kill the villagers?"

The others were silent, watching as OarsumBoss destroyed the rest of the vegetable gardens and then moved toward the nearest hut.

As OarsumBoss reached the hut

the door opened and a villager appeared. OarsumBoss swished his sword back and forth. The villager sidestepped the sword, threw a potion at OarsumBoss, and hurried back to his hut.

"Oh no," Jamie groaned. "He's probably poisoned Sam."

"At least it stopped him from hurting the villagers," Annie said.

"We need to go in and see if we can save him," Jamie said. "We can't risk him coming home and telling our parents. And we know him well enough to be sure that's exactly what he'll do."

JJ turned to Annie. "If he dies you'll need to go down to the forest and stop him. Convince him to wait for us before he comes back to the house, tell him we know a way he might be able to go back into the map."

"Do we?" Annie asked.

JJ shook his head. "No, but he doesn't know that. You just need to buy us some time so we can come back out and talk to him."

Annie frowned. "Okay. But what if he's doing something evil? Should I try and stop him from out here or would it be better to just change the map?"

JJ nodded. "Yes, if it's a complete disaster change the map to the theme park one. That should definitely stop him and we know we can use the portal there to get home."

"If we realize something terrible's going to happen we'll use a signal so you know to change maps," Jamie said. "How about if we want you to change the map JJ and I stand facing each other? If we have swords, we'll put their tips together. If we don't, we'll just use our hands."

Annie nodded. "That sounds easy enough to remember."

Jamie grinned. "Awesome." He turned to JJ and Charli. "Everything's sorted, let's go."

JJ and Charli followed him out of the house and down the backyard to the forest. Jamie ran along the narrow path, across the creek bed, and up into the clearing that housed the portal. Its glowing purple light and welcoming hum greeted them as they slowed to a walk and caught their breath.

"Come on, there's no time to waste," Jamie said. He joined hands with JJ and Charli and pulled them into the portal, through to another world.

CHAPTER TWO

The Red Devil

Sam stumbled away from the village, his legs trembling as he tried to continue. His plan to show the villagers that he was boss had backfired. He hadn't expected them to be so clever. He groaned and leaned against a tree. His vision was blurred and the energy had drained from his body. He needed to eat in order to restore his health but he didn't have the strength to open his inventory. Sam's body crumpled over. He barely registered the thump as he fell to the ground. Was this what it felt like to die? Would he still be alive in the real world? Perhaps he should have waited for his cousins after all.

∽

The blocky Minecraft world unfolded in front of them as JJ and Charli sprinted after Jamie. There was no sign of Sam. They slowed to a walk when they reached the outskirts of the village.

Charli gasped as she looked toward the once-abundant vegetable gardens. "Oh no. He's destroyed it all."

JJ shook his head in disbelief. "There is so much work required to fix the gardens. We'll need to help them. Come on, first we have to find Sam."

The door of a hut opened as the three friends searched the village. "Jamie, JJ, Charli!"

"It's Toby," Jamie said, and hurried over to his villager friend.

"We've been attacked by an intruder, the Red Devil." Toby pointed to the vegetable gardens. "He destroyed all of our crops and was about to kill us, but my uncle stopped him. Poisoned him. Hopefully killed him."

"Do you know where this Red Devil is?" Jamie asked.

Toby pointed to the outskirts of the village. "He went that way, but he's probably dead. It was a strong potion."

"Come on," JJ said. "We need to hurry and find him."

"But why?" Toby asked. "You aren't planning to help him, are you?"

"It's a long story," JJ said. "We'll find him first and then come back and explain."

Toby nodded. "Okay, I'll wait here for you. But don't bring the Red Devil back. My uncle will be sure to kill him if he comes again."

"Let's split up," Jamie said. "Each of us can search a different area. He wouldn't have been able to sprint. He might be on the ground somewhere, like I was when Toby's uncle poisoned me that time." Jamie thought back to the horrible effects the potion had on him. He'd felt so weak, so helpless.

After they'd searched for a few

minutes Charlie's cry rang out from a group of trees. "He's over here!"

JJ and Jamie rushed over to Charli. OarsumBoss lay on the ground at her feet. His eyes were shut and he wasn't moving.

JJ nudged him with his foot. "Sam, can you hear me?"

A tiny murmur escaped Sam's lips.

"He's alive," JJ said. "But only just. Let's get some milk into him, see if that helps at all."

Jamie punched his left arm and his inventory pad appeared. He selected milk and threw it onto Sam. The milk disappeared as soon as it touched OarsumBoss' skin. It took a few moments before he started to move. His eyes opened and he slowly sat up. Using a tree for support, he pulled himself to his feet.

"Are you okay?" Charli asked.

"I'm really weak," Sam said.

JJ opened his inventory and threw out a cake. "You need to eat. The milk will only remove the effects of the potion. It won't restore your hunger."

Sam scooped up the cake and ate it. "Wow, this is delicious. Who would have thought you could actually taste it?"

Jamie grinned. "Awesome, isn't it."

Sam nodded. "Other than nearly dying, everything's awesome."

"You've really let us down, Sam," JJ said. "First you came in without us, ignored all of our rules, and then you attacked the village. Those villagers are our friends. You've destroyed their crops. What food do you think they're going to eat now?"

Sam laughed. "Who cares? They're villagers. They're not real like us. They don't end up in the real world if they die, do they?"

"This *is* their real world," Charli said. "If they die here that's it, they're gone forever just like you would be gone if you died in the real world. You have to respect their world if you are going to be in it, not destroy it."

"She's right," JJ said. "You can have a great time in here but you don't need to go around smashing or killing things, especially people, such as the villagers, who are a lot weaker than you are. They don't have the same sorts of weapons as us. It's not a fair fight."

"Not fair at all," Jamie said. "If you want to kill things wait until nighttime comes. There will be zombies, creepers, and endermen. Your Minecraft skills will definitely come into play. You don't need to kill innocent villagers. If you go back to the village now, the villagers will kill you. If they do you won't be able to come into the Minecraft world again."

Sam nodded. "Okay, so what next? Show me something exciting."

"We will," JJ said. "But first we're going to need to help fix the vegetable gardens you destroyed." He opened his inventory. "I've got seeds and bone meal. I think we should repair the damaged areas and then make the whole garden bigger. It might help make up for what Sam's done. Has anyone got a hoe?"

Jamie and Charli checked their inventories and shook their heads.

Jamie grinned. "Nope, so let's make one. Show Sam how it works."

"I know how to make a hoe," Sam said. "I said show me something exciting."

JJ winked at Jamie and Charli before turning to Sam. "How about you make us a hoe, Sam. You'll need to make a crafting table first."

They watched as Sam opened his inventory. He selected wooden planks and moved one into each of the four crafting squares. A crafting table appeared in the box next to the crafting squares and he used his finger to move it into his inventory. He looked up, his mouth set in a smirk. "Easy, how about you give me something challenging—"

Sam's words were cut off as dust swirled around their feet. The wind strengthened, blowing them back and forth.

"What's happening?" Sam shouted above the howl of the wind.

Jamie grinned. "Just wait and see!"

They were forced to shut their eyes as the dust thickened and the wind lashed around them. Then, as quickly as it started, it stopped. They opened their eyes. In front of them stood a crafting table with nine holes.

Sam's eyes widened as he stared at

the crafting table. "That was awesome. How does it do that?"

"We don't know," JJ said. "We just know that's how we get a crafting table and now we can craft anything we don't have, like a hoe." He opened his inventory. "I've got plenty of blocks of wood and sticks, so this will be easy." He selected the items they needed and threw them out of his inventory onto the ground near the crafting table. Jamie picked up the blocks of wood and put them into the first two holes of the table. He added the wooden sticks to the fifth and eighth holes. Immediately the wind whipped up again and dust flew everywhere. The crafting table rose up off the ground, spinning faster and faster.

JJ smiled as he watched OarsumBoss' mouth drop open in amazement. He needed to close his mouth before it filled with dust. They were all forced to close their eyes as the elements lashed against them once more. Suddenly the calm returned. A hoe now floated above the crafting table.

OarsumBoss shook his head. "That was sick. Can we craft something else? TNT maybe?"

JJ looked toward the horizon. "The sun's beginning to set so mobs will be out soon. If you want to kill something, nighttime will be your chance."

Sam grinned. "Awesome, I'll make TNT and blow them up."

JJ took the hoe from above the table

and added it to his inventory. "Okay, but for now let's fix the village, get the crops growing again, and move away from this part of the map. We can hunt for mobs somewhere where we aren't putting our friends in danger."

"What about the crafting table?" Sam asked. "Should we take it?"

"Just leave it," JJ said. "They're easy enough to make if we need another one."

Jamie, Charli, and Sam followed JJ as he moved back to the village. He stopped on the outskirts and faced Sam. "Wait here. The villagers are upset with you and you won't be safe if you re-enter the village. We'll fix their crops and then we'll all go and have fun somewhere else, it won't take long."

Sam opened his mouth as if to object but seemed to change his mind. Instead, he nodded and leaned against a tree.

"Come on." JJ led the way toward the vegetable gardens. He glanced over his shoulder and checked that Sam was still by the tree.

Charli turned her head to follow JJ's gaze. "He's actually listened for once. Being poisoned was probably the best thing for him. It seems to have given him a fright. Hopefully he'll listen to us from now on."

"Let's hope so," JJ said. "Now, quick, let's get to work before the sun sets. We haven't got long."

Sam watched as JJ, Jamie, and Charli hurried to the village's vegetable gardens. Jamie and Charli quickly went to work fixing the areas he had destroyed while JJ used the hoe to prepare the ground for the garden expansion. It was a large area to cover which gave Sam plenty of time.

He moved out from the tree and back to the clearing where the crafting table sat. He opened his inventory and grinned. He had masses of gunpowder and sand. He moved the ingredients he needed out of his inventory and onto the ground near the crafting table. He selected the items, carefully placing the gunpowder in holes one, three, five, seven, and nine. He placed the sand in the remaining holes. At once the dust whirled around his feet, the wind blowing from side to side as the crafting table shook and then spun high up into the air. Sam squeezed his eyes shut and waited. In no time the elements calmed and he opened his eyes.

A single block of TNT floated above the crafting table. He'd done it. Sam's heartbeat drummed in his chest as he added it to his inventory and set about making more. He glanced toward the village. His cousins weren't going to tell him what to do. Those villagers poisoned him. He'd show them all who was boss when he got his revenge.

JJ watched as Jamie and Charli added the third round of bone meal to the crops.

The vegetable gardens had been repaired and the crops were almost full grown. The villagers would be eating from them again soon.

"We're done." Jamie wiped the sweat from his brow. "Hopefully the villagers won't be mad at us."

"They won't be." Toby's voice caused them all to turn. "Thank you, my friends. You've saved us."

JJ laughed. "I don't think repairing the garden counts as saving you."

Toby shook his head. "You have given us extra crops and more food than we have ever had before. Last time your lava traps saved us from nighttime attacks by zombies, this time you've repaired the damage the Red Devil caused and ensured we will not starve. We have so much to thank you for."

"We like to help when and where we can," Jamie said. "There's no need to thank us."

Toby's smile disappeared. He pointed to the far side of the village. "The Red Devil is still here. He may destroy more of the village."

JJ looked to where Toby pointed. Sam was no longer by the tree, he was laying something along the ground and moving toward the village huts.

"What's he doing?" Charli asked.

They watched Sam take a block from his inventory and place it near one of the huts. He placed another, and another.

"He's laying TNT," Jamie said.

"Quick, we need to stop him before he blows up the village."

"There's no time," JJ said. "He's already placing a lever."

❧

Annie wiped the strawberry jam from the side of her mouth and eyed the plate of croissants. She'd already had two, did she have room for a third?

Her eyes moved back to the screen, she expected to see JJLee45, JamieG14, and Charli9 still at work in the vegetable gardens. Instead, JJ and Jamie stood facing each other with the tips of their swords connected. Her hands trembled. It was the signal. Something was wrong. They needed her to change the map. She fumbled with the controller and scrolled through the list of maps looking for the theme park one. It had an easy-to-access portal which would provide an exit to the real world. She found it and tried to select it. It was only as the map loaded that she realized her error. She'd selected the one above the theme park. The map loading was not one the Crafters' Club had ever gone through the portal to visit. She immediately made the decision to exit again and select the right one. She pressed the button on her controller but nothing happened. She pressed again. Nothing. She tried pressing other buttons but still, nothing. Her controller had frozen.

Sam turned his focus from the TNT to the redstone fuse and lever. He finalized the lever and placed it on the ground. His heart thumped with excitement as he looked toward the village. Villagers moved between the huts and the vegetable gardens. He rubbed his hands together. He'd laid enough TNT to blow up the entire village. All he had to do was flick the lever. The only problem was his cousins and Charli. He hadn't planned to blow them up but it was quite likely they'd get caught in the explosion. They'd assured him they wouldn't die in the real world, just the Minecraft world, so it wasn't such a big deal. The upside was that if they were gone they wouldn't be able to ruin his fun.

Sam turned to look at his cousins one last time. He hesitated. JJLee45 and JamieG14 stood facing each other, the tips of their swords touching. He shook his head, he had no idea what his cousins were doing, but it didn't really matter. He had a job to do and he wasn't going to be distracted.

Sam took a deep breath and stretched his hand out toward the lever. Before his hand connected, the ground beneath him rumbled and then shook violently. He gripped onto a nearby tree as the wind whipped up and thrashed against him. A lump caught in his throat as the world around him started to spin.

CHAPTER THREE

The Swamp Biome

JJ's stomach churned as he twisted through the air. Wind and dust thrashed at him as the Minecraft world spun. He was relieved Annie had seen the signal and changed the map. Groans sounded around him as he crashed to the ground and the elements finally calmed.

"Where are we?" Charli coughed. "I can't see anything."

"Me either," Jamie said. "Are we in the theme park map?"

JJ was relieved to hear the voices of his brother and friend, he just hoped that Sam had been transported with them.

"Give the dust and smoke a chance to clear," he said.

They waited. Charli drew in a breath as the world returned to normal. The boys were silent as their eyes adjusted to their new surroundings. They were not in the theme park map. They'd landed on the muddy bank of a swamp.

A scream rang out from behind them, breaking the silence. They leaped to their feet and turned to see Sam being attacked by a spider.

JJ watched as his cousin backed away from the creature. Why wasn't he slashing at it with his sword? Sam turned from the attack and sprinted toward them, the spider in close pursuit.

Jamie moved between Sam and the spider, his diamond sword outstretched. Two swipes and the spider died, leaving string and spider eyes in its place.

Sam let out a deep breath. "Thanks, that was freaky. I didn't expect the mobs to be so big, or so real." He looked around. "What happened, how did we end up here?"

JJ and Charli joined them. "Annie changed the map from the Xbox," JJ said. "We had to stop you from destroying the village. You would've killed everyone... You gave us no choice."

Sam shrugged. "But why here?" He looked around. "Where are we?

JJ shook his head. "Something's gone wrong. Annie was supposed to take us to the theme park map. There's a portal there that we know takes us back to the real world. Instead we're in a swamp. We need her to change the map again. Let's do the signal, Jamie."

"Okay." Jamie turned to Sam. "Be prepared, we'll be thrown all over the place again."

JJ and Jamie faced each other, put the tips of their diamond swords together, and waited.

Annie watched as JJ and Jamie faced each other, the tips of their swords touching. She tried the controller again but nothing happened. She pushed a hand through her hair. What should she do? If they were all playing out here on the Xbox they would restart the console. But they'd never done that with any of them in the Minecraft world. What if it killed all of them? Anything was possible, she knew that. She shook her head. She couldn't risk it. She'd just have to hope they'd work out that something was wrong and find their own way home.

There was no rumbling of the ground, no wind whipping up around them or spinning of the Minecraft world.

"Nothing happened," Sam said. "Nothing at all."

JJ removed his sword from Jamie's. "No, something's wrong. Annie wouldn't have sent us here on purpose. We're going to have to find our own way out. Let's move away from the swamp and see if we can find an area to build a portal. Hopefully it will take us home or to a map we recognize."

"Let's explore first." Sam pointed across the swamp. "I want to have a look in that hut."

JJ shook his head. "No, there could be all sorts of danger around. You don't want to come face to face with a witch. That spider scared you enough. We need to get out of here."

"No way," Sam said. "I'm not going anywhere. You promised me a Minecraft adventure and I'm not leaving until I've had an awesome one."

JJ bit the inside of his cheek as his anger boiled. "We might have promised you a Minecraft adventure but you promised you'd listen to our rules and respect the people and world in here. Instead you've terrorized our friends, destroyed their crops and buildings, and threatened to blow them up."

Sam snorted. "Whatever. I'm going to explore and there's not a lot you can do about it."

"We're not going to help you," Jamie said. "If you get into more trouble you're on your own."

Sam shrugged. "I'll be fine. I can look after myself."

Charli laughed. "Like you did with that spider? You're not as big and tough as you make out. You'll be lucky to last five minutes in here by yourself."

Sam's eyes flicked around his surroundings. "I can't see any more mobs. Look, I'll come with you after I do one last thing."

"Depends what it is," JJ said.

Sam shook his head. "You really don't get it, do you? It wasn't a question, I'm telling you I will do one more thing *then* leave the map with you." He pointed to the hut in the middle of the swamp. "That would look awesome if it exploded, don't you think?" Sam didn't wait for a response. He pushed Jamie out of the way and walked toward the hut.

"Idiot," Jamie muttered.

"Do we just let him go?" Charli asked. "What if he blows it up?"

"We really don't have much choice," JJ said. "We'll have to watch him, help him out of trouble if he gets into any."

"What? Babysit?" Charlie's yellow face broke into a wide smile. "I love it. Big, tough OarsumBoss needs a babysitter." She laughed. "Guess he's really showing us who's boss."

Sam moved away from his cousins and their friend. They were annoying. Why couldn't they just let him do whatever he wanted? Blowing up that village would have been awesome, but no, they'd had to stop him. They'd better not stop him from blowing up the hut. There would be trouble if they did. He glanced behind him. They hadn't followed, just watched from the edge of the swamp. Damp soaked through the legs of his red pants as he waded across the shallow water. He hoped it wouldn't get too deep. He wasn't sure how to swim in here.

He neared the hut. All was quiet. There was no witch. JJ was probably just trying to scare him. The hut was perched out in the middle of the swamp by itself, it would be awesome to fill it with TNT and watch it explode.

Sam reached the hut and hauled himself up a ladder to the doorway. He peered inside. A crafting table stood close to one wall but, otherwise, it was empty. He opened his inventory pad. He'd fill the room with TNT then run blocks, with a redstone fuse on top, down the ladder and across the water to where the others stood. They could watch it explode with him.

He started placing the TNT blocks. He turned to place a final block before running the redstone and stopped. His legs trembled as his gaze connected with another pair of eyes. He fumbled with his inventory pad, he needed a weapon.

It was too late, the crooked-nosed creature in front of him cackled and laughed. He'd invaded the home of a very real, very alive, witch.

Sam moved back, hoping to escape

the hut before the witch harmed him. She cackled again and punched the side of her hut. A hole opened up. Inside, Sam could see a large black pot, its contents bubbled as steam poured out the top. Pains gripped his stomach as he stared at the witch. He'd already dealt with the effects of one potion today, he really didn't want to experience another. He continued to shuffle back toward the door. Other than her terrifying cackle, the witch hadn't moved. Maybe she wouldn't?

He placed one foot outside the hut and froze. The witch cackled again and pulled a glass bottle from behind her back. Purple and blue liquid swirled around in it and bright pink smoke puffed from its top. Before Sam had the chance to react the witch took a step forward and threw the potion at him.

❦

The three Crafters' Club members remained by the side of the swamp, their eyes fixed on the witch's hut.

A few minutes had passed when JJ pointed. "Look, there's Sam."

They watched as OarsumBoss moved into the doorway of the hut, his back to them. He stood stiffly, as if he were frozen. Without warning he turned and fell face first into the swamp. His body floated on top of the water.

Jamie immediately stepped toward the swamp. JJ put a hand out and grabbed his arm.

"Stop." He pointed to the hut. The doorway had filled with the purple cloak, black hat, and squashed nose of a witch.

Charli's hand flew to her mouth. "Has she killed him?"

"No, he wouldn't still be floating if he were dead. He would have disappeared, leaving just his inventory. She's done something to him," Jamie said.

"Probably a potion," JJ said. "We need to get to him before it kills him."

"But what about the witch?" Charli asked. "She might come after us."

"I think we'll have to take our chances." JJ looked back up at the hut. "She's gone back inside. Hopefully she'll stay there. I don't think she saw us."

"Come on." Jamie led the way into

the swamp. They moved with caution toward Sam's floating body. Jamie reached him first and turned him over.

"If this were real life he'd be drowned by now," JJ said. "It looks like he's been poisoned again. We'd better give him more milk."

Jamie opened his inventory and selected some milk. He threw it on Sam. The body of OarsumBoss twitched but then stilled again.

"It must be a really strong potion," Charli said. "What do we do now?"

JJ looked up at the witch's hut. "Let's drag him back over to the bank. We can't risk the witch throwing a potion on all of us. We'd be in real trouble then."

They grabbed hold of OarsumBoss

and, between the three of them, dragged him through the water and back to the muddy bank of the swamp.

"Shouldn't a poison potion have worn off by now?" Charli asked. "He hasn't moved at all since we threw the milk on him."

"He twitched," Jamie said. He prodded his cousin with his foot. "He's really out of it. Let's throw a splash potion of healing on him, see if that does anything." Jamie opened his inventory. "I haven't got any splash potions, have any of you?"

JJ and Charli checked their inventories.

"I've got a potion of healing, but not a splash potion," Charli said. "There's no way he'll be able to drink it in this state. We'll need to turn it into a splash potion."

"Good idea," JJ said. "We'll need to make a brewing stand."

"I've got a blaze rod," Jamie said. "And cobblestone. First we'll need another crafting table."

He opened his inventory and dragged a wooden block into each of the four crafting squares. The wind picked up immediately and their surroundings blurred as mud spattered against them. The elements were quick to settle and a crafting table appeared.

"Perfect," JJ said. "Now add the blaze rod to the second square and cobblestone to squares four, five, and six."

Jamie rolled his eyes as he added the

items to the table. "I know how to make it. I've done it a million times."

"Here it goes," Charli called. A thunderous roar of wind whirled around them as the crafting table rose into the air and spun. The sky darkened as the wind lashed back and forth.

Charli grabbed onto JJ's arm. "I'm going to fall!"

JJ held onto her, trying to steady them both as the elements continued to smash against them. Finally the winds died and the crafting table settled back on the ground, a brewing stand next to it.

"Far out," Jamie said. "That was epic. I thought I was going to be sucked up with the crafting table and spun into another world."

"We've never had to make a brewing stand before," JJ said. "At least we know what to expect next time. Now let's make the splash potion."

Charli added the potion of healing to one of the bottom boxes of the brewing stand and then added gunpowder to the top. They stepped back and covered their mouths as the potion bubbled and white smoke poured from the stand. A red potion appeared. The smoke disappeared and the bubbling stopped.

Charli took the potion from the stand and threw it on Sam. He groaned and moved his legs. Then, once again, he stilled.

"Wow, whatever the witch has thrown on him is really strong," JJ said.

"Hopefully it will wear off soon. For now, let's build another portal and get out of here."

"What about Sam?" Charli asked.

"If he hasn't woken up then we'll drag him through the portal," JJ said. "It might be the only way to get him home."

"We'd better hurry, unless you're in the mood to fight some mobs," Jamie said. "It's going to be dark any minute."

JJ looked around. Jamie was right. The sun had almost disappeared below the horizon. They'd had plenty of practice building portals. It wouldn't take long at all. "Come on then," JJ said. "Let's get it built and get out of here."

Annie's stomach rumbled as she continued to watch the happenings on-screen. She picked up the Xbox controller again but was still unable to do anything. She sighed. It was a nightmare every time they entered the Minecraft world. They hadn't had one successful visit yet. A faint smile played on her lips as she thought about the near disasters they'd had. While they'd nearly died many times, had to flee from mobs, rescue each other, and exist in a world that appeared to have no rules, it hadn't all been a disaster. They'd made wonderful friends and the adventures, while unpredictable and scary, had turned out alright so far.

She reached for a croissant as she watched Charli throw a potion at Sam.

There was no point in being worried and hungry. The potion didn't appear to work. She wondered what they would do next. The sun was setting and a creeper was moving around the edge of the swamp toward them. Her heart pounded. A movement at the witch's hut caught her eye. She moved forward on her seat to get a better look. The witch was moving down the ladder. Was she planning to attack? JJ was laying obsidian as Jamie and Charli watched him. None of them seemed aware that danger was approaching.

JJ placed the last block of the portal. Now all they had to do was light it, drag Sam through, and hope they ended up back in the real world, or at least in a familiar map.

"Ready?" he asked.

Jamie nodded.

The pink smile on Charli's yellow face turned to a frown. She pointed behind JJ. A creeper stood on the other side of the portal. A hissing noise erupted from it and it began to flash.

"Run," JJ yelled.

They turned and ran. JJ grabbed one of Sam's arms and dragged him, as best he could, along the ground, away from the portal and creeper. A huge explosion threw him off his feet and into the air. He landed with a thump. Jamie and Charli landed close beside him.

"Jeepers, that was close," Charli said.

Jamie grinned. "Jeepers creepers, you mean."

"Not funny," JJ said. "We were almost killed and the portal's gone out." He pointed to where the new portal had been built.

Jamie laughed. "It was funny. We weren't killed and it will only take a few seconds to re-light the portal. Relax, would you?"

JJ looked at Charli and shrugged. Very little appeared to worry Jamie. If a creeper exploding that close to them didn't scare him, then probably nothing would.

"Is Sam okay?" Charli asked.

They looked over to where Sam lay on the ground.

"He's not dead yet," Jamie said. "So that's a good sign, I guess."

"He's moving his legs." Charli pointed. "Look."

They watched as Sam moved his legs, then his arms. He groaned and sat up. JJ, Jamie, and Charli hurried over to him.

"Are you okay?" Jamie asked.

Sam rubbed his head. "I'm not sure. What happened?"

"Which bit?" Jamie said. "The bit where you tried to blow up a witch and got poisoned? Or the bit when we were almost all killed by a creeper exploding?"

"I guess that covers it," Sam said. He looked at his cousins. "Hey, I'm sorry I didn't listen. This place is kind of scary. Can we go home?"

"We wouldn't be in this mess if you'd done what we asked to start with," JJ said. "We could have had some fun. Now we're stuck in a swamp. We'll re-light the portal and try to get out, but I can't promise you where it will take us."

Sam's face glowed the same brilliant red as his pants. "Sorry guys. I thought I knew better than you. How's this for a deal. I promise I'll listen to you from now on. You're the boss, not me. Just get me out of here and take me home."

JJ nodded. Finally his cousin seemed to be talking sense. He'd love to make him apologize to Toby and the villagers, but for now the apology to them was enough. They needed to concentrate on working together and getting home.

"Okay, first step is the portal. Jamie, why don't you re-light it while Charli and I look out for mobs."

Sam cleared his throat. "I'll look out for mobs, too. Why don't we all guard a different direction while Jamie lights it."

"Okay," JJ said. "You stay in front here, Charli and I will take one side each. Everyone will need to keep an eye out behind the portal, too."

They all took their positions as Jamie lit the portal with his flint and steel.

"Let's go," he called to the others.

"Grab hands," JJ said. They moved back in front of the portal's crackling light. "We want to make sure we all end up in the same place."

They linked hands.

JJ took a deep breath and put one foot forward, expecting to be sucked into the portal. He felt himself freeze. Something was wrong. He didn't feel right. He had no time to ask the others if they were okay. Everything went black.

CHAPTER FOUR

Annie's Test

Annie's hand flew to her mouth as she watched chaos unfold on the screen. They'd re-lit the portal but none of them had noticed the witch approach from behind. Just as they'd gone to step into the portal she'd crept up and thrown a potion over all four of them. They now appeared to be frozen. The witch had dashed back to her hut.

Annie hardly breathed as she willed them to move, to do anything. But they all remained still. It had taken Sam ages to regain consciousness after he'd fallen from the witch's hut. The potion was very strong.

Annie picked up the controller, praying it would work. It didn't. She debated what she should do. Should she go into the Minecraft world and try to save her friends and Sam? There was no guarantee she'd end up in the same map as them and definitely no guarantee she'd be able to access inventory or do anything to help. Perhaps she should just wait. The potion would wear off and then they could come through the portal on their own.

A movement to the left of the screen caused Annie to stifle a scream.

An enderman lurked in the shadows by the swamp. What if it saw them? What if it tried to kill them?

The decision was made for her. There was really no choice. She couldn't let her friends die in the Minecraft world, not without a fight at least.

She leaped from the couch, dashed through the house and down the yard to the forest. In what felt like only moments she arrived at the portal, panting, and out of breath. There was no time to stop and think through a plan. Annie took a giant step, straight into the portal's shimmering light.

Annie's eyes adjusted to the darkness that surrounded her when she arrived as CakeGirl1 in the Minecraft world. She needed a diamond sword and armor, now. She checked her inventory and her heart sank. It was empty. A lump formed in her throat and tears welled in her eyes. She shook her head, angry with herself. She would not cry. She'd come to save her friends and she needed to think fast. She didn't even know if she was in the same map as them.

She moved forward, her eyes scanning her surrounds. A flicker of purple caught her attention through a group of trees ahead. She continued toward them. The lump in her throat dissolved as she saw the glimmer of the portal. On the other side of the portal was a swamp. Relief calmed her nerves. She was in the same map. She moved closer. The four bodies of JJLee45, JamieG14, Charli9, and OarsumBoss lay on the ground. They were all still.

Her eyes darted around. They'd been blindsided by a creeper and the witch. She couldn't let the same thing happen to her. The enderman she'd seen from the Xbox was still slinking around the side of the swamp. Her heart rate quickened as she recalled her last encounter with an enderman. Sure, she'd won the battle, but she'd had full diamond armor and a diamond sword. This time she didn't even have a cake to throw at it. She looked again at her friends. Perhaps she could drag them one by one through the portal? She shook her head. There was no guarantee she'd be able to get back to this map if she did that. She needed to restore their health so they could all enter the portal together.

The enderman was getting closer. Annie didn't look, she knew better than to make eye contact. But the *crunch-crunch* noise was unmissable.

An idea came to Annie. With her heart in her throat she squeezed her eyes shut and prayed for a miracle. She opened her eyes and got to work. Jamie's was the easiest body to access. She lifted his arm and punched it twice. She'd only ever accessed her own inventory, she had no idea if this would work. She waited.

Nothing happened.

Annie dropped Jamie's arm and kicked out in frustration. Her foot connected with Jamie's other arm. She pulled it back, horrified at what she'd done. "Sorry, Jamie," she said. She hoped he hadn't felt that. Jamie's arm shook and his inventory pad appeared. Annie moved closer to access it. She shook her head, glad that the others hadn't seen her first attempt. They'd be laughing at her for trying the wrong arm.

The inventory pad opened. Annie let out a breath, there was plenty of inventory to choose from. She selected armor and a weapon. The items floated in front of her. She was quick to put on the diamond armor and took the diamond sword in hand. She was ready in time, but only just.

The *crunch-crunch* noise was closer, much closer. Annie turned, careful to keep her eyes low and not look directly at the enderman. She had a job to do and didn't want it to teleport. It had to be killed so she knew it was gone. The *crunch-crunch* noises were replaced by its terrifying scream as the enderman attacked.

Annie launched at it, swinging her sword back and forth. The enderman hissed and screamed as it attacked but Annie stood her ground. She cut at its legs again and again. Its terrifying noise increased in volume and Annie knew this was a sign that it was in the throes of death. With one final slash of her sword, all went quiet. The enderman was dead. An enderpearl hung in the air where it had been. Annie collected it and scanned the area for mobs once more. The area surrounding her was still. There was no activity or noise to suggest mobs were about. Annie took a deep breath and looked back at her friends. Still no movement.

She looked across to the witch's hut, it was dark but she could make out the faint outline of the building. Smoke streamed from the roof. She imagined the witch was in there making more potions. Should she be doing the same? Making a potion of healing to help everyone? She could, but what if the witch threw one of her own on all of them as they tried to leave, like she'd done before? No, that wasn't the answer. The witch needed to be destroyed. It was the only way to guarantee their safety.

❧

Annie was pleased she'd thought of a plan. The problem now was the detail. Yes, she needed to destroy the witch, but how? She'd seen Sam filling the witch's hut with TNT. She wasn't sure how he'd planned to ignite it. A redstone fuse was no good. It wouldn't work over water or up the ladder. She could lay blocks first but she didn't like the idea of moving that close to the hut.

She needed another plan. She hadn't had a lot of experience with witches when playing Minecraft but she was pretty sure that a lot of the ways to kill mobs didn't work on them.

She checked Jamie's inventory again and selected some food. She ate a cake to ensure her hunger bar was full. It was delicious. She'd like another but her hunger was full now and she needed to concentrate on the rescue mission, not on her stomach.

She thought back to the one time Jamie had shown her through a swamp biome. He'd killed three witches, all with a bow and stack of arrows. He'd explained to her then the problem with witches. They had stronger health than most mobs and were immune to potions. In fact, some of the potions that should kill mobs only acted to strengthen witches.

She reopened Jamie's inventory. His weapons were mainly swords, there was no bow. She moved around to JJ and opened his inventory pad. He had an arrow but no bow. She frowned. What use was an arrow without a bow? She took the arrow and moved on to Charli. Charli's inventory was full of cakes, swords, and potions. No bow. Annie's heart sank. It only left Sam and she doubted he would have anything useful. She opened his inventory and scrolled through his items. It amazed her how well prepared he was. He appeared to have nearly every inventory item available. Had he really gone to the trouble of organizing that much inventory before he snuck into the Minecraft world? From the look of his inventory he could have been in creative mode, not survival. Excitement flooded through her as she looked at his weapons. Not only did he have bows, he had enchanted ones, too.

Annie selected a bow enchanted with infinity. She had the arrow from JJ's inventory, and one arrow was all she would need.

The sky lightened as Annie secured her weapons. Relief washed over her. Nighttime was over. She preferred daytime. The mobs didn't seem as scary and there weren't as many about. She hoped she would only be battling the witch and nothing else.

As the sun rose she had a clear view to the horizon. On the side of the swamp, closest to the witch's hut, was a group of gravel blocks. Annie moved toward them. Hopefully they would give her the protection she needed. Now all she needed to do was get the witch's attention.

⚬

Annie found a spot behind the blocks. There was a crack between two just wide enough for her to be able to get a clear vision of the witch's hut, even when she was crouched down, out of sight. She selected the enchanted bow and an arrow from her inventory. She took a deep breath, opened her mouth, and yelled. "Hey, witchy! Come out and play."

She ducked back behind the blocks. The witch had not appeared. Annie stood up and called out, her voice even louder than the first time. She crouched back down and waited.

It worked. The witch appeared at the door of the hut. She looked from one side of the swamp to the other. Having not seen anything she turned back as if to re-enter the hut. Annie screamed out again and ducked back behind the blocks.

The witch spun around. Her purple cape flapped and she pulled out a bottle and drank from it before moving down the ladder toward the swamp.

Annie realized immediately what the witch had done. She'd drunk a potion to protect herself. Annie hoped that wouldn't work against the arrows. She needed the witch to get closer before she could fire. She called out again, watching as the witch reached the swamp and began to wade through the water toward the bank.

Annie watched, her heart pounding as the witch moved closer. She was about to stand up and take aim when another voice rang out.

"Look out, the witch is coming."

It was Sam. Annie peeked her head over the block high enough to see Sam standing near the portal with JJ next to him. Jamie and Charli were still lying on the ground.

"Grab Jamie," JJ yelled. "I'll get Charli. We need to drag them into the portal and get out of here before the witch gets us."

Annie stood up from her hiding spot. She drew the bow to eye level and loaded the arrow. She pulled back and fired at the witch. Immediately the bow reloaded with another arrow. She released it, not even taking the time to see if the first arrow had hit.

JJ grabbed Charli's arm and dragged her toward the portal. He looked back to check that Sam had Jamie. He did. The witch was almost at the edge of the swamp and they needed to leave before she had the chance to throw another potion on them. It was pure luck the first one had worn off. He waited for Sam to catch up.

"Come on, hurry up," he said. He watched as Sam dragged Jamie across the ground toward him.

Sam stopped suddenly, dropped Jamie's arm, and turned toward the witch.

JJ followed his cousin's gaze. The witch was under attack. Arrow after arrow flew at her. She screeched and cried as each arrow lodged in her body. JJ looked back to where the arrows were flying from. He grinned. He couldn't believe it. CakeGirl1 was attacking the witch.

"What's happening?"

JJ looked down as Charli moved. She pulled herself up off the ground and stood next to JJ. Jamie was moving, too, and now stood next to Sam.

"Annie's come to save us," JJ said.

"From the Xbox?" Charli asked.

JJ nodded. "She must have got it working again."

"So we can all go through the portal then," Charli said.

Jamie turned to her. "Yes, but we have to watch this first. Don't forget, we promised Sam an adventure and I reckon seeing Annie firing arrows at a witch counts for that." He slapped his cousin on the arm. "What do you reckon, pretty cool, eh?"

Sam nodded. "Sure is. Look, she's killed the witch."

The arrows stopped flying as the witch, with a final screech, disappeared. Glowstone dust, gunpowder, and sugar hung in the air where she had been.

"Okay, we can go," Charli said.

"Shouldn't we say hi to Annie first?" Sam said.

Charli laughed. "She can't hear us if she's on the Xbox. Let's get home, you can say hi to her there." She put her hand out for Sam to take and the other for Jamie. "JJ, grab onto Sam, let's go home."

The four friends joined hands. As they stepped toward the portal a voice rang out from behind them.

"Hey, wait for me!"

They stopped and spun round. CakeGirl1 sprinted toward them.

"I thought you said she was out on the Xbox?" Sam said.

JJ shook his head. "I thought she must be."

"I can't believe you were going to leave without me." Annie arrived in front of the group.

"We thought you were playing on the Xbox," JJ said. "I'm so sorry."

Annie smiled. "That's okay. The main thing is the witch is dead, the mobs are dead, and it's time to go home. Come on, let's go."

The five Minecraft characters, JJLee45, JamieG14, CakeGirl1, Charli9, and OarsumBoss grabbed hands and, without hesitation, stepped into the portal's flickering purple light.

CHAPTER FIVE

Back in the Real World

Raindrops sprinkled down on the Crafters' Club members and Sam as they tumbled out of the portal and onto the soft grass of the forest.

"We're back," Sam said.

They all looked at each other. Wide grins filled their faces.

Jamie flung his arm around Annie's shoulder. "You saved us. You are absolutely amazing."

"You sure are," JJ said.

Annie's face turned pink. "I just did what any of you would have done."

"I don't know," Charli said. "I'm not sure I would have been able to kill the witch like you did. How on earth did you get the arrows firing that way?"

Annie grinned. "You can thank Sam for that."

"Sam?" the others asked.

"Me?" Sam said. "How do you work that one out?"

Annie explained that she'd arrived without inventory and had to use the inventory of the others. "So I checked your inventories and except for the one arrow JJ had, none of you had anything I could use at all. Except for Sam, his inventory was amazing. It had nearly everything you could think of in it. How did you do it?"

Sam shrugged. "I just loaded in anything I could think of before I went in, like you said we needed to do." He grinned. "I did listen to some of your instructions, you know."

The four Crafters' Club members laughed.

"Anyway," Annie continued. "Sam had a bow enchanted with infinity so it was easy. I just got the witch to come out of her hut and killed her."

"Amazing, Annie," JJ said. "You've proven again and again that we can rely on you to get us out of trouble."

"Yes, you're awesome, Annie," Sam said. "I caused lots of trouble today and thanks to you everything is okay. First you changed the map so I didn't do damage to the village and then you came and saved our lives. What can I do to thank you?"

Annie grinned. "Nothing. Just be a nice person, don't try and take over, and hang out and have fun with us."

"Really?" Sam said. "That's all you want from me?"

"Of course," Annie said. "That's all any of us want. JJ and Jamie would love to be friends with you and include you in things." She turned to the two boys. "Wouldn't you?"

They nodded.

"You've just got to be one of us, not boss us around or be nasty," Jamie said.

Sam nodded. "I can do that. You guys

are cool. Really cool, in fact. This was the most exciting day of my life and thanks to Annie I can do it again. I didn't die in there so we can have more adventures."

"I'm not sure about that," JJ said. "Today was pretty dangerous. Maybe tomorrow we'll go to the movies or something."

Sam laughed. "Whatever you say, JJ. I'd love to go back into the Minecraft world but if we don't go tomorrow then we can go another time. For now let's all treat Annie like the hero she is."

Annie blushed an even brighter red as the other four cheered, high-fived, and clapped her on the back.

Jamie lay in bed thinking about the adventure they'd had. Even though for part of it he'd been affected by a witch's potion and unable to do anything, it was still awesome. He smiled as he thought of Sam and how his cousin had started the day being so boastful and breaking all the rules, compared to the end when he celebrated Annie's bravery and agreed to join in and follow the club's rules.

He listened to JJ's steady breaths in the bunk above. He'd never had a chance to check if JJ really meant it about the movies. He didn't want to go to the movies, he wanted to go back into the Minecraft world. He considered waking his brother up to ask him but changed his mind. He had to remind himself that sometimes, even though JJ was older, he wasn't the boss.

No, he wouldn't ask JJ's permission to do anything. In fact, he had a better idea. He crept out from under his covers and tiptoed to JJ's room, where Sam was sleeping. He opened the door quietly and snuck inside.

"Sam, are you awake?"

There was no response.

He increased the volume of his whisper. "Sam, wake up."

The blankets rustled and Sam sat up. "What? What's wrong?"

Jamie moved closer and sat on the edge of the bed. "Nothing's wrong, I just wanted to have a chat."

"About what?"

"About the Minecraft world. I think we should go back in."

"But what about JJ? He said we couldn't."

Jamie gave a soft laugh. "Are you for real? Smart, tough, OarsumBoss is going to listen to my ten-year-old brother?"

"He won't let us," Sam said.

"He can't stop us," Jamie replied. "There's something I've always wanted to do and the others are too chicken. I think you are the perfect person to share this adventure with."

Sam nodded. "Okay, I'm in. What are we doing?"

"Tomorrow you and I are going to the End and we're going to meet the ender dragon."

"Really? Meet the ender dragon?"

Jamie grinned. "Did I say meet? I meant *defeat* the ender dragon."

Books currently available in The Crafters' Club Series

Two Worlds, The Villagers, Lost
The Professor, Spirit, Friendship
The Secret, The Promise, The End.

Sneak peek of book nine, The End

Attempting to travel to the End brings unexpected mob encounters, heart-stopping battles, and an extremely difficult decision for Jamie and Sam. Overcoming these challenges is only the first step. If they are successful they will face the hardest task of all. Kill the ender dragon, or be defeated and never again return to the Minecraft world. Do the Crafters' Club members have the skills to complete their mission and live to have another Minecraft adventure, or is this really the end?

Visit TheCraftersClub.com to purchase The End and other titles in The Crafters' Club Series. Alternatively, chat with your favorite book retailer.

Join The Crafters' Club – It's Free!

You too can join JJ, Jamie, Annie, and Charli as a member of The Crafters' Club. Prizes, special offers and advance notice of new book releases are just some of the benefits of belonging to the club. Sign up for free today at:

www.TheCraftersClub.com

Acknowledgments

Thank you to Ray and our two boys for their knowledge and instruction on all things Minecraft. Without your interest and enthusiasm The Crafters' Club would not exist.

Thank you also to all of the members of The Crafters' Club for your emails, letter and messages. It is wonderful to receive your feedback and hear what you love about the characters and series.

A very special thank you to Minecraft fans, and avid readers, Finn and Rocky, for their feedback on early drafts of the story. To Judy, a huge thank you for your well-utilized proofreading services.

Sincere thanks to Kathy Betts of Element Editing Services for your thorough editing and improvement of this story and the entire Crafters' Club series.

Finally, thanks to Lana Pecherczyk for her cover design, and to Navid Bulbulkja for his fantastic character illustration.

Made in the USA
San Bernardino, CA
16 January 2018